The Edge of the Hunter

Steampunk OZ: Book 8

by Steve DeWinter

I0625871

Summary

In this action-packed second season of Steampunk OZ, American author S.D. Stuart returns to the Australis Penal Colony, where an ancient, and devastating, weapon was hidden a millennium ago.

Book 8

After being captured, Caleb agrees to retrieve the weapon for a new enemy. But will he turn it over to save his own skin, or does he have another plan?

This book is a work of fiction. References to real people, events, establishments, organization, or locales are intended only to provide a sense of authenticity, and are used fictitiously. All other characters, and all incidents and dialogue, are drawn from the author's imagination and are not to be construed as real.

Ramblin' Prose Publishing

Copyright © 2014 Steve DeWinter

All rights reserved. Used under authorization.

www.stevedw.com

eBook Edition

ISBN-10: 1-61978-046-1

ISBN-13: 978-1-61978-046-0

Paperback Edition

ISBN-10: 1-61978-047-X

ISBN-13: 978-1-61978-047-7

Chapter 1

Caleb stood before the mahogany desk in the Captain's private stateroom aboard the airship. He been stripped of his suit of armor for the second time and wore only leather pants and a rough cotton shirt. If it were not for the fur over his entire body, the shirt probably would have itched.

What did itch was the stiff metallic collar they had placed on him. He fidgeted with it uncomfortably.

Levi, the leader of the Directors' advance army, sat at his desk ignoring Caleb. He spun the key he had liberated from Nero in his fingertips, inspecting every centimeter of its brass surface.

Levi was dressed like a Roman Centurion, ready to lead his troops into battle. Only it wasn't his troops he was sending into battle. It was Caleb.

There was a faint knock at the door right before someone poked their head in. "We just crossed over the border into the Northern Territories."

Levi set the key down on the leather-topped desk. "Any indication we've been spotted?"

"None, sir. As far as the grounders are concerned, it's blue skies all around."

"Good. Take us to the city Nero identified and prepare to touch down."

"Yes sir." The man disappeared, closing the door behind him.

Why would Nero be helping someone who thought of himself as an elite soldier from an extinct civilization? The world had moved on. Humanity had progressed. Yet, this man dressed as if he was still in Rome a thousand years ago. He even made his private army dress the part. Caleb chuckled to himself. The only reason they likely ever won in battle was that the enemy was laughing too hard to fight.

Levi eyed him suspiciously. "I know what you're thinking, but Nero is not helping us as much as he's just trying to stay alive. And I suggest you do the same."

"Or what?"

"That is not for me to decide. I am not the judge. Only the executioner."

"So if I refuse to help you with your plan, you'll kill me?"

"We are not the savages you believe us to be."

"Anybody who wants to use that weapon against anyone else is nothing but a savage."

"You're forgetting to see the good in people. With that device we can…"

Caleb felt compelled to correct Levi's misconception of what it was they were after. "Weapon."

Levi took a deep breath before continuing. "With that device, we can bring about a level of peace the world has experienced only once before. The same kind of peace that existed when your kind had the device, and used it to keep everyone in line. We only wish to recreate the world as it was so long ago. A world free from war. Free from hatred. Free from violence. Peace is the gift we want to give to the world."

"And they want to use the most destructive weapon ever created to bring this peace?"

"If it could be done any other way, we would gladly do it."

He had heard enough and was not convinced. "Then you'll just have to do it without my help. You can torture or kill me if you want to."

"I have no intention of harming you. At least not yet. But I will not hesitate to hurt the girl. What was her name? Oh, yes. Dorothy."

His heart stopped. She was not with him in the warehouse when Levi blew it up. There was no way he could find her, let alone hurt her. He was bluffing.

Levi smiled. "You think I'm bluffing. What would you say if I told you that I would hurt her terribly if you do not cooperate? And the man in the wheelchair who was with her."

But how? How had they found her? OZ was a big place. It was an entire continent! Yet Levi had come directly to them, when they could have been anywhere.

Levi seemed very pleased with himself as he settled back into his chair. "You think Nero would send you out on such an important task without a way to keep track of you? Like I said, he has been very helpful in finding you. Just as you will be very helpful in finding the boy who hid the device."

"What makes you think I'll help you?"

"Along with the leverage I have over you by keeping Dorothy here, safe with me, you're not going into the city alone."

The door creaked behind him, signaling someone entering the room. Levi smiled. "And here is your partner now."

Caleb half turned when a fist slammed into the side of his face. The unexpected attack sent him down to his knees. He looked up into the face of Captain Taylor. Surprisingly, Taylor extended his hand and helped Caleb back to his feet. What was Captain Taylor doing with Levi?

"I thought you worked for the Southern Marshal," Caleb said.

"I work for whoever's going to win. And Levi convinced me that she did not stand a chance against what's coming."

The truth suddenly dawned on Caleb, like the sun breaking through storm clouds. "You helped them escape from her dungeon."

Taylor beamed with pride. "And get their ship back." Taylor looked at Levi. "See, I told you it wouldn't take long to bring him up to speed. He's one smart cookie."

Levi leaned forward, his elbows resting lightly on the desk. "And you think you can keep him under control?"

Taylor pointed to a small box, with a single button on it that sat on the desk. "As long as I have that, it won't be a problem."

Levi pushed it over to him and Taylor snatched it up before it flew off the edge of the desk.

Taylor held it up and showed it to Caleb. "I bet you're wondering what this is."

In fact, he had been wondering what it was.

"I could go into a lengthy scientific explanation about what it does, but it would be faster to show you."

Taylor pushed the button and it felt like fire ignited in his neck and tore through every muscle in his body. He reached for his neck and gripped the collar, the source of the electrical surge. In no time, he was on the floor writhing in pain.

The pain suddenly stopped and he gasped, as he lay there, helpless.

Taylor bent over him. "You will do exactly as I say or I will rest a heavy rock on that button and let that collar cook you from the inside out."

Caleb panted heavily as he lay on his back, unable to respond. That satisfied Taylor, who returned his attention back to Levi.

"I don't think he'll be a problem, sir. We will find the boy and get back what he stole from you."

Two hours later, Caleb and Taylor stood in the middle of a marketplace in the Northern Territories. According to Taylor, this was the same marketplace the Totos had been following Jasper. Since he did not have access to the Toto network, Taylor insisted they wander around the marketplace and wait for Jasper to walk past them.

Caleb wore a hooded cloak to hide his feline features. After the mass exodus to the south, there were no hybrids anywhere else in OZ. If someone spotted him, it would draw unwanted attention. Fortunately, for him, the Northern Territories were not a friendly place and people ignored each other quite readily. Everyone, except for one man who called out to every potential customer who came within earshot of him.

As the two of them worked their way through the marketplace, keeping an eye out for Jasper, he could hear what the huckster was saying as they got closer.

"Only sixpence a try. Bring your key, any key. Every key in your house. Be the one to unlock the mystical, magical box and claim the treasure waiting inside."

Caleb shook his head. Leave it up to Jasper to figure out a way to make money from a locked box. He pointed the huckster out to Taylor.

"I think we found it."

Jasper tossed another farthing to the bartender. "Keep those sarsaparillas coming."

The bartender looked at him with his good eye, the non-milky one, while he slid the dirty coin across the counter and poured two fingers of the sweet drink into Jasper's glass. "If this keeps up, I'm going to have to cut you off."

Jasper snatched the glass and hovered over it like a dog protecting its dinner. "There's no alcohol in this."

"True, but if you're throwing farthings on the bar, you're almost out of money."

Jasper stared down at his reflection in the brown liquid. Being able to read people must be one of the prerequisites to becoming a bartender.

Separated from Nero, and with the rest of the army dead, he found himself in a strange land with no money. In addition, who was going to hire a young kid for anything, and pay him? He had to do something that would give him the freedom he wanted, and the money he needed.

He instantly fell back on some of the scams he pulled off back at home, but quickly realized the inhabitants of the Northern Territories were a much tougher crowd. The still tender burn, from a hot poker pressed into the palm of his right hand, attested to that.

None of his old tricks were going to work here. He needed something new. Something that wasn't perceived as a scam, yet could still provide him a steady income.

Nero's box proved to be the perfect answer. If Nero could not open the box, with his vast resources and knowledge, what chance did anybody else have?

So, why not let everyone have a try? Let them bring their own keys and pay for the chance to get at the treasure inside. A locked box holds a secret. Everyone loves a secret. It proved to be the perfect money-making scheme.

For about three days.

Now it seemed that this town's interest in a locked box had waned and he was down to a few farthings in his purse. It was time to take his box to another town. And next time, he would conserve his money.

Randall sat down heavily next to him at the bar, his face beaming. "I got two more takers for you," he said as he nodded toward the door of the tavern. Two men stood at the entrance, one of them wearing a hooded cloak.

Jasper's suspicious nature took over. They certainly didn't look like the usual clients willing to pay for an attempt at the unknown. They must be up to something.

He didn't take his eyes off the men as he probed his assistant, who was many years older than he was, but none the wiser, for more information. "How many keys?"

"Just one."

He rubbed the last of his two farthings in his pocket between an index finger and thumb. This wasn't sounding too good. "Did you tell them the sixpence price is for a bulk discount?"

"I did. They agreed to the one try for three shillings."

"How much convincing did it take?"

"I should have asked for a whole pound, because they agreed right away."

This was sounding too good to be true. From his experiences growing up in OZ, anytime it was too good, it wasn't true. His suspicions were all but confirmed and he couldn't let his overwhelming need for money override his finely tuned survival instincts. He knew when not to get sucked into a trap.

"They're not customers, Randall. Send them away."

"No, no. They are customers." Randall held out his open hand, three shillings clinking together in his palm. "They've already paid. See?"

Jasper snatched all three shillings from Randall's hand. No sense in letting money go to waste.

"Fine. But take them by Draco first. He will determine if they are customers or not."

Jasper grabbed Randall's collar and pulled him back to the bar as he started to walk away. "You can forget about your cut if he kills these two like he killed the last one. We don't need the kind of attention another body will bring. The townspeople are already spooked that there might be a monster running around loose, and if there is another victim, there will be far too many guards posted around the city for us to continue our business arrangement."

From across the room, Caleb watched Jasper control the conversation between him and Randall.

Taylor leaned over and whispered, "Is that the kid we're looking for?"

Caleb nodded silently.

It certainly looked like Jasper. But he behaved very differently than he had ever seen him behave before. In fact, if he didn't know better, it looked as if Jasper was acting like a crime lord. But he did know better. He knew Jasper, and he was no crime lord. Sure, he ran his fair share of scams, but what kid growing up in OZ didn't? It was a dog eat dog world, and now, Jasper was acting like the biggest dog of them all.

Randall shook himself free from Jasper's grip and rushed over to them. "Okay, it's all set. Follow me."

They followed him out of the tavern, Caleb taking the opportunity, as the door opened, for one last glance at Jasper. His seat at the bar was already empty. Caleb looked around the tavern, but Jasper was gone. This was not a good sign.

Once outside, he had to run to catch up to the others. Taylor was already engaging Randall in conversation.

"Is it far?"

"No, no. It's close."

Randall seemed exceptionally nervous. Another bad sign.

A few minutes later, Randall slipped into a side alley that ran between two multistory buildings. The space between the buildings was so small, Randall had to angle his body sideways just to fit.

He craned his neck back and waved them in. "This way."

Caleb and Taylor exchanged a look. They would have to enter one at a time just to fit.

Taylor took a step back and thrust a hand into his pocket, most likely resting a finger over the button of Caleb's electric shock collar. "After you."

The space was too small to make a move against Taylor anyway, so he angled his shoulders and stuffed himself into the tiny crevice.

It was a tight fit. The mismatch stones of the walls tugged at his cloak and pulled back his hood, exposing part of his face.

Halfway down the alley, Randall stopped at a door set into the side of one of the buildings. A look of horror crossed his face when he noticed Caleb was not human.

He fumbled the key into the door as Caleb inched his way closer. Randall disappeared and the door slammed behind him.

Caleb reached the door and twisted the knob, but it was locked from the inside.

Was this part of their plan from the beginning?

Or did Randall panic when he saw Caleb's face?

Either way, the door was locked and they were wedged into a very tiny space.

Taylor grunted behind him. "Don't just stand there, open the door."

Caleb rattled the door handle. "He locked it."

Taylor shifted around uncomfortably. "Don't toy with me."

"I'm not."

The sound of rock grinding on rock was accompanied by the wall pressing Taylor into the building behind them. He shot forward to join Caleb in the doorway. Within moments, the alley was completely sealed and they were both crammed together into a tiny space.

Their faces so close, Caleb winced at Taylor's hot breath as he spoke. "If I wasn't touching you, I'd shock you so hard for getting us into this mess."

The door flung open and they both fell into the room, Caleb falling onto his back with Taylor landing on top of him. A shaft of light pierced the hazy darkness from the single window on the high ceiling. His earlier guess at this being a multistory building was incorrect. It was tall, but the one room stretched from the ground all the way to the top of the building.

Caleb's enhanced vision enabled him to see in the semi-darkness. The only door out of this room was the one they had come in. And now, the walls of the alley had sealed that up, leaving no way out.

The rustling of chains brought his attention back to the center of the chamber as a large half-human half-lizard creature stepped into the shaft of light. His wrists were bound by chains that stretched to twin holes in the wall behind him, but the chains were still long enough to give the creature free rein over half the chamber. Fortunately, it was the other half of the chamber from where Caleb and Taylor slowly picked themselves up.

Caleb had seen every type of hybrid imaginable back in the Southern Territories. But they were all mammal based. This is the first one he'd seen that was reptilian.

The creature held on to his chains and tugged at them, unable to get any closer. It let out a mighty roar that nearly emptied Caleb's bladder. He had been trained as a master assassin since before he could walk and feared nobody and nothing.

Until now.

Nothing in his training or experience prepared him to stare into the cold eyes of a reptilian hybrid. There was no doubt that if the reptilian hybrid were not chained to the wall, he would've already torn them to shreds without emotion or remorse.

A clanking sound emanated somewhere deep within the opposite wall. The reptilian hybrid responded by spinning around and pulling as hard as he could on the chains. It didn't do any good and he was pulled back to within a foot of the wall before the chains stopped retracting into the holes.

A deep voice echoed to them from the darkness above. "Why are you interested in the box?"

Before Caleb could respond, Taylor was already talking. "You enticed us with your sales pitch."

"But you had only one key, and you didn't negotiate."

"Where I'm from, money is not a problem. Your price sounded very fair."

"Do you know what is inside?"

"We were hoping to find that out when we opened it."

"How do you know your key will unlock the box?"

Caleb placed a hand on Taylor to stop him from responding and took over the negotiations.

"You tell Jasper that I have Nero's key."

The room fell silent, except for a faint snarling and the rustling of chains from the other side of the room.

After a moment, a more familiar voice echoed from above. "Caleb?"

Finally, a friend.

"Hello Jasper."

There was a sound of rocks grinding on rocks and stairs began to form that led to a niche high up along one wall. Jasper appeared and rushed down the stairs. He charged at Caleb and embraced him in a huge bear hug.

"It's so good to see your friendly furry face."

Caleb hugged him back. "I missed you too."

Jasper looked around, ignoring Taylor. "Where's Dorothy?"

Taylor, not wanting to be ignored, replied for him. "We have her."

Jasper frowned. "What do you mean, 'you have her'?"

"She will stay safe as long as we get what is inside that box."

Jasper jabbed a thumb at Taylor. "Is he with you?"

Caleb half smiled. "Not exactly."

Taylor took a step forward. "He is my prisoner. You will take me to the box at once."

Jasper crossed his arms. "Or what?"

Taylor glanced sideways at Caleb. "Or I will make him suffer as no one has suffered before."

Jasper glanced around him and laughed. "And just what can you do down here? You don't exactly have the home field advantage."

Taylor removed the small box from his pocket. "This button controls your friend's shock collar. If I hold it down long enough, his heart will stop and he will die."

Before Jasper could respond, a grinding sound drew their attention to the stairs receding back into the wall.

Jasper called out, "Randall, what are you doing?"

Randall appeared at the niche in the wall, "What I should have done a few days ago when you first approached me with our deal."

Gone was the stuttered and slurred mumblings of the simpleton. Instead, it was replaced by the eloquent speech of a mastermind criminal. "You have a very unique scam there, Jasper. I think I can do a lot with that. Thank you for your contribution."

His disappearance through the niche was followed by a hollow thunk in the wall behind the reptilian hybrid. All three of them looked over as the hybrid pulled on his chains, testing to see if they would pull farther out of the wall.

Which they did.

Jasper swore and sat down roughly on the floor in defeat. "I can't believe I fell for the oldest trick in the book. Scam the scammer. I thought he was a simpleton. It's a shame I won't be around to tell my grandchildren about the best scam ever pulled on me. I'm not even going to be around to have children."

Caleb grabbed Jasper and pulled him back to his feet. "How do we get out of here?"

Jasper stared right through him, lost in his own thoughts. "We don't. I don't know if you noticed the grates in the floor. That's for our blood to drain away after the lizard man eats us."

Caleb tossed Jasper into the corner and then whipped off his hooded cloak. They had one chance to survive this and he didn't need that heavy cloak getting in the way.

"Taylor?"

Taylor was staring at the hybrid, frozen like a statue.

"Taylor!"

Taylor's head jerked in his direction.

"Get ready to trigger my shock collar."

Taylor gave him a quizzical look. "What?"

"As soon as I grab the lizard, you trigger my collar."

The reptilian hybrid kept pulling the chains out of the wall until they ratcheted to a stop. The chains were now looped at his feet, and looked long enough to let him reach anywhere in the chamber.

He was eyeballing the three of them, trying to decide which of them to save for dessert.

It was now or never.

Caleb shot a sideways glance at Taylor. "Get ready."

Taylor snapped out of whatever he was thinking and shouted.

"Wait!"

"No time!"

Caleb leaped through the air. The monster responded in kind and met him in the middle of the chamber in midair.

They collided heavily and fell to the ground with a thud. Caleb struggled against the powerful strength of the creature and screamed over his shoulder. "Do it now!"

For some reason, Taylor did not trigger the collar.

On his back, he gripped the monster's arms and pushed up against the sharp lizard claws as the reptilian hybrid pushed down on him with all his weight. Caleb craned his head over to look at Taylor. "Do it!"

Taylor responded, "I can't. There was only enough power for one shock."

The truth that his collar was a one-time scare tactic was information he would've liked to have had before formulating his hasty plan. The reptilian hybrid was bigger and, he was quickly discovering, stronger than he was. Taylor was useless, but Jasper jumped to his feet and yelled something absurd as he ran by. "Just hold him there Caleb. I have an idea."

The reptilian hybrid's sharp talons were getting closer to his face. "I think you've underestimated my position here, Jasper."

His muscles screamed with fatigue as one sharp talon pierced his cheek, blood bubbling up through his fur. Pain shot through his whole body. As soon as he couldn't resist any longer, the hybrid would slash through him with razor-sharp talons and then quickly finish off Taylor and Jasper.

Of all the ways Caleb had envisioned his death, he never imagined it would be at the hands of another hybrid.

The monster was suddenly jerked backward out of his grip and flew away from him. Jasper was just rolling to the side, and barely missed being crushed, when the hybrid impacted with the wall. He collided with the wall with such force, it crumbled inward. As the dust settled, they could see the reptilian's lifeless legs poking out, half buried in rubble, from the newly punctured hole in the wall.

Jasper was back on his feet and dusting himself off. "I almost forgot about the chain retraction switch. I didn't think we'd be able to get past the lizard to activate it."

Caleb shot to his feet and pinned Taylor against the wall. "This whole time, the collar was useless?"

Taylor smirked. "The threat of violence is far more coercive than the act of violence itself. Besides, we still have Dorothy."

Despite Taylor's attempt at bravado, Caleb could smell the fear emanating from his pores. There were many things he wanted to do to this man, but he was right. The threat of what they could do to Dorothy would keep him in line.

Jasper tugged on his arm. "Caleb. We have to get out of here. Randall helped me find some people to guard the box. I should've trusted my instincts, but I didn't know anybody here. He acted so... I thought he was simple. We have to get there before he moves it."

Caleb ignored him and held his face close to Taylor's and bared his fangs. "If anything happens to Dorothy, I will tear you apart."

Jasper pulled harder on his arm. "Caleb. Caleb!"

Caleb spun on Jasper. "What!?"

Jasper flinched, but held his ground. "If you want to get the box before Randall moves it, we have to go now."

Taylor spoke up. "I thought you said there was no way out?"

Jasper pointed to the new hole in the wall. "There is now."

Jasper disappeared through the hole that led to the inner workings of the chain assembly. It took only a few turns through the labyrinth behind the hybrid's feeding chamber to reach the door at the other end of the twisting tunnel. Jasper paused at the door and waited for them to catch up.

"The box is just on the other side of this door, unless Randall has already moved it." He looked at Taylor. "You really think you can open the box?"

Taylor responded immediately. "We have the key and a flask of Dorothy's blood to activate the lock. We can open it."

"A flask of her blood?" Caleb gripped Taylor's collar. "I thought we needed Dorothy to open it?"

Taylor shook his head. "The key has needles that extract blood from the person using it. You hold this flask in your hand, and the key won't know it's not Dorothy."

Why hadn't he thought of that? He could've left Dorothy with the Southern Marshal. Then she never could've been used to control him. She would have been safe.

Jasper nodded his head and pushed on the door handle.

Nothing happened.

He pushed harder. "The door's stuck."

"It's locked?" Caleb asked.

"No. There's no lock on this door. There's something wedged into the frame on the other side. Help me push."

The three of them leaned their shoulders into the door and slowly pushed it. It popped open, the small piece of wood that had been used to jam the door clattered across the floor.

This chamber was nearly identical to the reptilian hybrid feeding chamber. It was a single, circular room that stood three stories high with a single square shaped opening at the center of the ceiling to let light in.

Jasper ran up to the table in the middle of the room. It was the only piece of furniture in the otherwise empty room. He slammed his hands on the empty table, dust rising up from its surface.

"It was right here!"

He continued to bang his fist on the table in exasperation when Caleb heard something strange coming from the hallway they had just been in. It sounded like the steady rush of air escaping a poorly sealed steam engine, only it was growing louder.

No. It wasn't getting louder. It was getting closer.

And the closer it got, the more he realized it wasn't a single sound, but a multitude of similar sounds happening simultaneously.

By the time the strange noise sounded like it was right outside the open door, it had attracted even Jasper's attention. "What is that?"

As if in answer to his question, hundreds of snakes flooded through the opening of the doorway, like honey forced through the nozzle of a syringe.

Chapter 2

The first wave of snakes writhed across the floor away from the door making room for the snakes being pushed in after them.

Jasper was already at the door on the far side of the chamber. It was the only other way out of the room. And the only way that wasn't filling fast with snakes. He slammed his whole body against the door repeatedly before giving up and running back to the center the room.

"It's locked from the outside."

A few snakes made their way to the center of the room and the three of them took turns kicking them away.

Taylor tucked his foot under the middle of a writhing snake and flung it across the room. "They're still coming through the door. How many of these things are there?"

Jasper kicked at, and missed, the two snakes bearing down on him. He hopped up onto the table to get away from them. "Enough to fill this chamber three feet deep in snakes."

Taylor joined him on the table. "That's way too many snakes."

Caleb leaped over the snakes as they slithered across the floor and landed on the table. It creaked under their combined weight, but held.

For now.

He looked into Jasper's eyes and saw only fear. "Did you know about the snakes?"

Jasper shrugged. "It's why I kept the box here."

Taylor crossed his arms. "Well, you're an idiot."

Caleb shot him an angry look. "We need to focus on getting out of here, now."

Taylor sneered at him. "I'm open to whatever suggestions you may have."

By now, there wasn't a single section of the floor not covered in snakes. And every minute another hundred were spilling in through the door. Above him, the opening in the ceiling beckoned. What he wouldn't give to have his flying suit right now.

The floor was a boiling mass of writhing snakes. There were so many, they filled the room halfway up the legs of the table.

The three of them were trapped, with no way out.

"Hey!" Taylor yelled as he shoved Jasper off the table. Caleb's reflexes kicked in and he snatched Jasper out of the air and pulled him back to the table.

He snarled at Taylor. "If somebody's going into the snakes, it's you."

Taylor jabbed a finger in Jasper's direction. "He hit me in the head."

Jasper puffed out his chest. "I did not."

"Something hit me in the head."

Just then, something bumped into Caleb's back. Thinking it was a jumping snake, he spun around and grabbed it, ready to throw it as far as he could.

Instead of a snake, his hand gripped a rope.

A rope that went up.

His eyes followed it up and out the square window in the ceiling.

Relief flowed through every muscle in his body.

Taylor pulled Caleb's hand off the rope and bumped him aside with his whole body. "Outta my way."

Taylor climbed the rope faster than Caleb thought was humanly possible without the benefits of hybrid strength and dexterity. When Taylor reached the top, he was pulled through the window by helping hands.

Caleb held his hand out to Jasper. "After you."

Jasper climbed just as quickly. The snakes, having reached to within an inch of the top of the table, were a great motivator.

Caleb didn't wait for Jasper to reach the top before pulling himself up the rope. He lifted his foot at precisely the same moment the snakes overran the table.

Chapter 3

Caleb clung to the rope as it was lifted through the hole in the ceiling. He was dangled a foot above the roof next to the Tin Man. In fact, it was the Tin Man who had pulled him to safety.

It was just the two of them on the roof. Jasper was already halfway up the ramp of the airship that waited on the far side of the roof.

The Tin Man lowered his arm, setting Caleb gently down. "Nero is tracking the box. We have to go before they take it underground and we lose it again."

Without a word, he followed the Tin Man up the ramp and into airship. As soon as he stepped off the ramp, two men pulled on the ropes to withdraw the ramp, and the airship throttled up into the air, gaining speed quickly.

As he turned the first corner, a strange sight greeted him. Two men were binding Taylor's hands together with rope and stuffing a gag into his mouth to silence him. More soldiers were tied up and seated uncomfortably along one wall. Some of them looked like they had fallen down a flight of stairs, or had been in a huge fight and lost.

"What's going on here?"

The Tin Man continued walking, ignoring the tied up soldiers. "We have regained control of the airship."

Levi, bound in thick rope at the front of the line called out, "For now."

The Tin Man brushed past him and into the control room. Caleb couldn't help smiling at Levi as he passed by.

If they could keep control long enough to destroy the ancient hybrid weapon, they would successfully derail the Directors' plans. But they had to get to the weapon first.

Inside the control room, Nero sat in the captain's chair. It was more accurate to say he leaned heavily to one side of the chair. The armrests were the only thing keeping him from falling to the floor.

His face was purple and bruised. One eye had swollen shut and a trickle of dried blood formed a crimson trail that led from one ear down into the open collar of his shirt.

He collapsed to the floor when he saw Caleb.

Caleb rushed up to him and lifted him back up into the chair. "What have they done to you?"

Nero's words came out mumbled and slurred. "Don't worry about me. Finish the mission. You are in command now, son."

Nero slumped into his arms.

The Tin Man immediately barked orders to those standing around in the command center. "Get Nero above deck and make sure he's comfortable. Caleb is now your commander. You will do as he says."

One of the command crew slipped his shoulder under Nero's arm and helped him out of the room.

All eyes fell on Caleb, waiting for him to say something.

Anything.

He was suddenly in charge, and they were all waiting for him to make a decision. He'd never been in charge like this before, and had no idea what to do, or say. But he did know one thing, they had to get the weapon before the Directors arrived in a few days.

He cleared his throat and everyone snapped to attention.

"Where…"

His voice cracked and he coughed to fully clear his throat again.

"Where is the box now?"

A crew member glanced at a readout on his control board. "It is to the east, and getting further away."

Jasper was at his side. "The northern entrance of Chambers is in that direction."

Caleb's brow furrowed. "Chambers reaches into the Northern Territories?"

Jasper nodded. "Chambers extends into all areas of OZ. If they take it in there, it could stay hidden underground forever. Or until they are ready to bring it back out."

"Then we get it before they go inside."

Jasper turned to the pilot." You heard the commander. Full speed ahead!"

The pilot spun in his seat and started punching buttons on the control panel in front of him. "Yes, sir."

The airship surged forward and pressed Caleb fully into the captain's chair.

Jasper regarded him with a faint smile. "You look at home in the Captain's chair. It suits you."

He shifted uncomfortably in the chair. "I don't know. I much prefer the silent stalking of my prey.

I'm used to working alone and only relying on myself. I still don't think I'm leadership material."

Jasper shrugged. "I think you've got what it takes."

The spotter, still tightly clutching the binoculars to his face and staring out the front window of the airship, called out. "Target in sight."

Caleb's hands gripped the armrests. "Can you see where they are headed?"

The spotter shifted his binoculars. "The entrance to Chambers is directly ahead of them."

He asked the next question he didn't really want to know the answer to. "How long?"

"At their current rate of speed, they will be at the gate in less than ten minutes."

He took several breaths to calm his nerves. They couldn't let the weapon disappear in to Chambers. They would never find it then. They would never be any closer to getting it than they were now. This was their one chance, and they had to take it.

Jasper touched his shoulder. "If you are going to do something, better do it now."

Jasper was right. If he was going to do anything, now was the time.

"What can this airship do?"

The weapons officer spun in his chair to face him. "We have forward facing cannons. We could seal the entrance before they get to it."

Jasper was shaking his head. "The people in Chambers are a bit defensive, for obvious reasons, but nobody has ever openly attacked them. There's no telling how they will respond. I say it's too risky."

He remembered that while growing up, even Nero spoke about the people in Chambers only in private, and even then, in whispers.

Nero, the man who never feared anything, seemed to fear them.

The spotter broke the silence. "They are getting closer, sir."

He looked from Jasper to the pilot. "Can we get ahead of them?"

"The best we could do is get there just as they enter," the pilot replied.

He looked back at Jasper who was shaking his head vigorously.

Making enemies was not something he wanted to do within the first few minutes of being in charge, but he also couldn't let the weapon slip from his grasp. Not when they were this close.

"I don't have a choice," he whispered to Jasper.

Jasper closed his eyes and let out a deep sigh.

When Jasper's older, he would understand.

"Ready the forward guns. Fire on my mark."

The weapons officer flipped several switches and positioned his hand above the launch button. "Ready on your mark, sir."

"Fire."

The weapons officer pushed down on the button.

Nothing happened.

The officer double checked his control panel and pushed the button again.

Still nothing happened.

"Two minutes to the entrance," the spotter called out.

Caleb sprung from the captain's chair and hovered over the weapons officer. "Why aren't we firing?"

The officer was frantically flipping switches and turning knobs before pressing the launch button again. "I don't know sir. The cannons aren't responding."

"One minute to the entrance."

They were going to lose the weapon.

They were going to lose everything.

Unless, they risked everything.

He was at the pilot's side. "How quickly can this ship be brought to full speed?"

"Within a matter of seconds, sir."

"So we could get to the entrance before them?"

"No sir, it takes longer to slow down. They would be inside before we came to a full stop."

"What if we didn't slow down? Could we reach the entrance before them?"

"Yes, but then we would shoot right on past it."

"Not if we were pointed directly at the entrance."

The pilot's eyes widened in understanding. That told him everything he needed to know.

"Do it."

The pilot turned to his control panel, his hand trembled as he reached for the throttle. "Yes, sir."

"They're almost at the entrance, sir."

He stood to his full height and said in his best commanding voice, "That'll be enough spotter, I have a new job for you. Get above deck and tell everyone to throw anything out of the ship that might be combustible, then strap down and brace for impact. You have thirty seconds."

"Yes, sir!"

As the spotter dashed out the door, Caleb was back in the captain's chair.

Jasper was tying himself down into a chair to one side. "You sure you know what you're doing?"

"I've seen my share of airship crashes. As long as we don't explode, we should live through this."

An alarm sounded followed by a calm prerecorded voice. "Warning. Collision detected."

Caleb strapped himself in as best he could and gripped the armrests.

"Okay pilot. Full speed ahead."

Chapter 4

Nelson cherished the days when his rotation schedule placed him guarding the entrance to Chambers in the Northern Territories. He spent so much time underground, his skin was pale and he found it difficult to adjust to the bright sun.

He wore dark goggles, so he could see in the daylight, and a full leather suit, complete with gloves, to protect his skin from the scorching rays of the sun.

Other than the threat of being burnt to a crisp by the fireball in the sky, guarding an entrance to Chambers was relatively simple. They had spread enough rumors topside to keep all but the most daring from even attempting to approach an entrance.

A typical day for Nelson was standing a few feet inside the cave entrance, away from the direct rays of the sun, and making up stories to tell young children around the dinner table about his exploits topside. As far as they were concerned, he was a valiant warrior who kept away all sorts of nasties so they could sleep safely each night.

Today, however, was not looking to be a typical day. For the last twenty minutes, he'd been tracking a small group headed for the entrance. The same entrance he was guarding. Today, his story around the dinner table might have a ring of truth.

They carried a large box that must have been heavy, because they slowed every couple of minutes to hand off the box to someone else in the group. The closer they got, the more often they alternated who was carrying the large box.

When he judged them to be less than a minute away, he pulled the double-barreled flintlock rifle from the gun cabinet. The cobwebs that clung to the barrel attested to how often he needed it. He blew off the cobwebs and dust and did his best to make it look like a serviceable weapon. The truth of the matter was, this gun hadn't been fired since before he was born, and most likely wouldn't work even if he tried.

In his experience, just telling someone he had it was enough to make someone think twice about forcing their way into Chambers. He'd never needed it before, and in fact, he had never removed it from the gun cabinet. Watching the group, as they made their way up the low hill, he was afraid that today would change all that.

Behind the group, a multitude of objects suddenly fell from the sky and hit the ground in plumes of raised dust. He glanced up to see the source of these objects and nearly wet himself.

An airship was headed straight for him.

And it was coming in fast.

Chapter 5

Caleb clenched his jaw as he pressed himself back in to the captain's chair. The view through the front windows showed the widening cavern entrance to Chambers.

It was a large cave opening, but not as large as the airship's rigid frame.

He yelled out to everyone, and no one in particular, "Hold on!"

The wrenching of metal grated at his ears as he was thrown forward against the straps of his chair. The front windows exploded inward, showering everyone with shards of razor-sharp glass.

It was over in the blink of an eye.

At least it felt like the blink of an eye.

He lifted his head and had no idea how much time had passed. Around him, the rest of the command crew all hung to one side of their seats, still strapped in. He knew they weren't dead because he could see the slight rise and fall of their chests. There was still life in every one of them. Relief washed over him. His first major command decision hadn't killed everyone.

The walls of the control room had buckled and pushed everyone closer together, but thankfully, nobody had been crushed to death. Moans coming from outside the command room reassured him that there were more survivors. It was quite possible that everyone had lived.

He sniffed the air, but found no indication that they were burning. The rigid frame of the airship had borne the brunt of the impact. The airship had stopped fast enough that only the front of the gondola was damaged. Everyone else inside was shaken, but safe.

He struggled against the straps, but the sudden impact had bent the lock mechanism and he was stuck. He raked his claws against the tightly woven fabric, shredding the strap in half to escape from the chair.

He fell sideways out of the chair and realized, a moment too late, the airship had come to a rest at a sharp angle to one side.

He stumbled and slammed into a side window that had somehow survived the initial crash, shattering it.

Stunned, and laying on his side, he saw leather boots stepping up into the broken gondola from outside the airship. He heard the click of a flintlock cocking lever lock into position and his eyes focused on the rifle barrel pointed directly at his face.

His view shifted down the long barrel and refocused on the dark goggles of the man aiming the rifle.

He sat up and the man instinctively took a step back while sighting down the barrel of his rifle. At this range, the man could not miss.

After a couple of attempts, Caleb finally found his voice. "Do not let the men with the box into Chambers."

The man with the dark goggles held the rifle steady. "Ain't nobody getting in or out of Chambers with what you just did."

He let his head drop back on to the shattered glass. "Good."

Goggles looked around at the destroyed airship. "Why did you do that?"

"Inside the box is a weapon. We have to get it away from the men who were carrying it. Can you help?"

Before Goggles could answer, the Tin Man smashed through the door of the command room, saw the rifle pointed at Caleb and swatted at Goggles with a metallic claw. The rifle flew from Goggles' grip and went one way while he landed on his back in the other direction.

The Tin Man towered over Goggles, one claw raised, when Caleb yelled out. "Don't!"

The Tin Man paused, his claw poised to come down at any moment and slice Goggles in half.

Caleb was back on his feet and shaking away the dizziness. "What are you doing Tin Man?"

The Tin Man stood stock-still, as only an automaton could. The only indication he was functioning was the crackle of his voice through his front speaker. "He shot down the airship."

Caleb picked up the rifle and held his hand out to Goggles. "Nobody shot at us. It was my decision to crash the airship."

He pulled Goggles to his feet and held out his rifle to him. Goggles looked from the rifle to the Tin Man, unsure of what would happen to him if he took the offered rifle.

Caleb smiled carefully, trying not to show too many of his sharp teeth in an effort to calm the man down. "Don't worry; I won't let him hurt you."

The move was so sudden; Caleb almost blinked and missed it.

The Tin Man's claw scissored right through Goggles' neck.

The shock of surprise was frozen on Goggles face as his head dropped from his body and rolled away across the floor. His body, now headless, buckled and collapsed to the floor.

The Tin Man swung around and pinned Caleb to the wall by his neck, the sharp blades of the claw shearing off bits of fur. The color of the Tin Man's single unblinking eye glowed a soft amber. "I do not take orders from anyone."

Chapter 6

Caleb's mouth went dry as he watched the blood from the decapitated guard drip down the edge of the Tin Man's claw. The monstrous automaton leaned in close. "Tell me why I shouldn't kill you right now."

He struggled to come up with some form of answer, but another voice broke the silence.

"What's going on?"

Still holding Caleb against the side of the airship hull, the Tin Man twisted his torso to see the new intruder.

Dorothy stood in the doorway with a puzzled expression on her face. "What are you doing to Caleb?"

It almost sounded like the Tin Man was amused at some private joke by the tone in his voice. "The question you should be asking yourself is, what was Caleb planning to do with us?"

If Dorothy's expression looked puzzled before, it was even more so now. "What are you talking about?"

The Tin Man's grip tightened on his neck as he spoke. "Who sent us on this expedition to locate and bring back the world's most destructive weapon ever created?"

Dorothy still looked confused. "The Southern Marshal."

"Wrong! Nero sent us out here. And who did he hand select to lead us?"

The Tin Man twisted back to stare at Caleb with that unblinking amber eye. "Nero is not to be trusted. You are not to be trusted."

He gripped the claw around his neck with both hands, lifting himself up to relieve some of the strain on his spine. "I was selected because I'm the chosen hybrid leader, not because of Nero."

The Tin Man did a very strange thing.

He laughed.

"All of the information we have on this weapon, its origin, its purpose, what it can do, everything we know, comes from a single source. Nero. His loyalty was always in question. And since your loyalty is aligned to him, your loyalty is in question. And you do not have the best track record."

He struggled against the claw as it tightened around his throat. "I'm not doing this for Nero. I'm not even doing this for the hybrids."

"Then why are you here?"

"I'm here for her. I'm here to help Dorothy."

The claw relaxed slightly and he coughed as he gasped for breath.

The Tin Man did not release him, but eased up the pressure on his throat a little more. "Explain."

"Nero and the Southern Marshal, they asked me to help. I was going to say no until I found out

Dorothy was going to come along. I came to protect her."

"And you've been doing such a wonderful job. You expect me to believe you have no interest in the weapon?"

He could barely shake his head, it was pressed so tightly against the bulkhead of the airship. "No. I'm only here because of her."

"If she were no longer part of the equation, would you still want the weapon?"

"No."

The claw tightened around his throat. "I don't believe you."

"It's true."

"Prove it."

"I don't know how to prove it."

The unblinking amber eye came within inches of his face. "I do."

The Tin Man pointed his other arm at Dorothy. The claw shot out, trailing a rusted chain. She did not have time to react before the claw clamped on her head, covering her face. The Tin Man yanked his arm backward and the unmistakable sound of Dorothy's neck splintering as it shattered from the twisting force echoed in Caleb's ears.

It took him a moment to realize the person screaming was him.

"Nooooo!"

The Tin Man retracted his claw from the lifeless Dorothy.

"Dorothy is no longer part of the equation. Do not follow me. I will not spare your life again."

He released Caleb and used his claws to tear through the side of the airship, and then he was gone.

Caleb stumbled across the uneven floor and picked up Dorothy, cradling her in his arms. Her head flopped awkwardly to one side, her eyes staring off into the blank space.

He slowly swiped his fingers across her face and shut her eyelids to let her sleep one last time. He cradled her head in one hand and held her close. Everything he had done to keep her safe. Everyone he tried to protect her from. But the one she needed protection from the most, had been by their side the whole time.

From outside he heard the reports of gunfire followed by screaming. And then silence.

The Tin Man had claimed more victims.

Chapter 7

The Southern Marshal instructed her pilot to land the airship a hundred meters away from the crash site.

Surrounded by twenty armed men, she picked her way through the dead bodies and up the hill to where two-thirds of the airship still stuck out of the cave at an awkward angle.

One of her soldiers vomited when his foot nudged a rock that turned out to be a severed human head. She looked more closely at the bodies scattered about. These were not victims of the crash. They had been killed after.

She'd never seen this kind of brutality before. Not even at night on a full moon. Whoever had done this clearly deserved to be in OZ.

A chilling thought ran down her spine. Whoever had done this might also have the weapon.

She gave the soldier with the weak stomach a stern look. He wiped his mouth and stood up straight. "Won't happen again, ma'am."

She bent down and rolled the head over to get a look at the face. The dead out here wasn't anyone she knew. They also didn't look like any of Levi's soldiers.

She pointed to several strategic points around them. "Set up a perimeter. I don't want anyone sneaking up on us while we inspect the crash.

Several soldiers barked a firm, "Yes, ma'am!" and ran off in different directions. It paid to have a well-oiled machine.

The soldier closest to the wreckage called back. "Survivors!"

Guns pointed at the airship as an access panel popped out from the side of the gondola and clattered to the ground.

The first person to drop out of the access panel was Levi. His shoulders dropped with a heavy sigh as he raised his hands. "I know, I know."

In three large strides, she was in front of him. "What happened here?"

He lowered his hands and shrugged his shoulders as he looked around. "This is what you get when you put a cat in charge."

"What?!"

"We caught up with your friends and captured them. Somehow, they managed to take control of the airship from my crew. I tell you, you can't get good help these days. Maybe when this is all over, you can tell me where you train your people."

He was acting more like a friend than a prisoner at gunpoint as he continued.

"Nero put that cat creature in charge, and the first thing he did was ram the ship into the side of a mountain. Nearly killed us all."

So, everyone was on the ship. "Where is he now?"

He hooked a thumb over his shoulder. "Probably knocked out in the command room. Idiot."

Without saying a word, her team understood her nonverbal commands and hauled Levi to the side, putting him with the rest of his soldiers as they climbed out of the airship. With so many guns pointed at them, they knew better than to try anything.

She had to get inside and talk with Nero.

She clambered up, grasping the handholds on the side of the gondola, and pulled herself up through the access panel.

She worked her way through the twisted wreckage until she reached the opening to the control room.

Just inside, Nero, Jasper, and Caleb stood over the body of Dorothy.

Caleb heard her come in and looked up briefly before lowering his head again. She could see the grief written in his face.

Nero's face was puffy and bruised. Nobody else looked as bad as he did, so his injuries were probably sustained prior to the crash. She would have to thank Levi for that later in her own special way.

She approached the small group. "Where's the weapon?"

Caleb moved so swiftly, she didn't have time to react before he had an arm under her chin and pinned her to the floor. "Is that all you care about?"

She struggled against him. "That's all that matters."

He fought back and held her down. "If you haven't noticed, one of the pieces of the puzzle is gone, forever. It doesn't matter where the weapon is now."

"Where is the weapon?"

"I think the Tin Man took it."

She stopped struggling and stared defiantly into his eyes. "Where is the key?"

Jasper spoke up. "The Tin Man said it would be safest with him."

She craned her neck to look over at Jasper. "And you gave it to him?"

He nodded.

She wanted to scream and lash out at the stupidity of everyone in the room. Instead, all she said was, "Then it's too late."

Caleb frowned at her. "Too late for what? Nobody can open the box without Dorothy, and she's dead."

She closed her eyes and imagined the worst. "There's something you don't know about the Tin Man."

Chapter 8

The Tin Man pulled the box that contained the ancient hybrid weapon deep into a cave, miles from the crash site. He set the box in a corner of the cave and settled down in front of it, illuminating it in the darkness with his amber eye.

A loud clunk echoed from deep inside the Tin Man, followed by a rush of steam that spewed from the crevice made when his back split open down the middle.

The steam quickly dissipated and human hands reached up to grab a pull bar situated just below the back of Tin Man's neck.

The arms flexed and the bar snapped down with a click. The occupant's helmet rose up, allowing a lock of soft curls to unfurl out the back of the Tin Man.

Dorothy stretched, flexing her upper back, first one way, and then the other. Her back responded with a series of pops.

Dorothy used her arms to pull herself out through the back of the Tin Man suit and dropped to the ground.

Her legs wobbled and she leaned heavily on the side of the Tin Man for support. Against the warnings of her father, she had stayed in the suit too long and her mind had adjusted to how she moved with the suit. It was like having to adjust to walking on dry land after having lived on a boat for a year.

She reached back up into the operator's compartment and withdrew the key Jasper had given her.

She stumbled around the front of the Tin Man and knelt in front of the box, casting a shadow over it when she came between it and the single point of dim amber light.

She spun the concentric circles embedded in the puzzle key until the letters spelled her last name in ancient Greek.

Needles protruded out from the handle with a snap and she gripped the key, grimacing slightly as they punctured the flesh of her hand.

She twisted the key in the lock and heard it engage, triggered by the blood running through her veins.

The lock sprung open and the lid popped up slightly with a faint hiss.

She rested her hand on the lid and felt heat emanating from the opening. She lifted the lid and peered into the dark box. For some reason, she had expected it to be glowing, much like the emerald heart her father had given her a lifetime ago.

Inside the box, was only darkness. She shifted slightly to allow the light coming from the Tin Man to reveal the contents of the box.

In the faint light, she could just make out the tip of something inside the box. She reached in and pulled out a tiny pyramid that rested lightly in the palm of her hand.

It was much smaller and lighter than she had expected, considering how big and heavy the box was that held it. She really hadn't known what to expect, but for some reason she thought it would be bigger. At least it should have been heavier.

She positioned it closer to the light and inspected it. It was a perfect little pyramid, complete with its own tiny gold capstone. All four sides leading down from the capstone were polished to a smooth finish except for a single groove closer to the bottom that ran along all four sides. Flipping it over to the bottom revealed the only stylized etching anywhere on the pyramid.

She angled it slightly to let the shadows fill the etched design. It revealed the picture of an eye with lines shooting out of it in all directions.

She traced the etched eye delicately with a finger. The center of the eye was made from a different material and looked like it could open with a spiraling motion like the iris of a picture camera. She dug at the center of the eye with her thumbs, but it refused to open. There must be a switch or lever somewhere on the pyramid.

With the exception of the etching on the bottom, the rest of the pyramid was as smooth as polished marble. The only thing different was the gold capstone on the top.

She gripped the capstone with the tips of her fingers and slowly twisted it clockwise. It refused to move. She twisted harder, but the capstone didn't budge. Maybe that wasn't the switch to open the eye. Or, maybe she was turning it the wrong way.

She gripped it again and twisted counterclockwise. It resisted slightly before starting to turn.

Intense pain shot through her other hand, the one spread across the base of the pyramid. She roared out in pain and dropped the pyramid, the capstone springing back to its original position. She had stupidly held her hand across the eye as she opened it.

She inspected her injured hand in the light. Her glove had deteriorated at the center of her palm. Despite being a new leather glove, it looked to be a hundred years old and was peeling apart.

She bit the tips of the fingers on her glove, and tugged it off her hand. The skin in her palm had blistered as if she had touched the business end of a white-hot fireplace poker.

She had barely turned the capstone. If this was what the weapon could do in the matter of a single second, when it was only partially opened, what could it do when it was fully opened?

She picked up the weapon again and turned it around in her hand. She had seen something that matched the same size and dimensions as the bottom of the pyramid before.

She turned around and stared at the small square panel set into the front of the Tin Man suit.

Now she knew where she had seen the exact same picture of the pyramid's eye before.

Inside the suit was a button with that same picture. She had pushed it before, but nothing happened.

She held the base of the pyramid up to it. It was exactly the same size.

With her gloved fist, she pounded on the faceplate. It popped off, leaving an inverse pyramid depression in the front of the suit.

She rotated the pyramid until the eye was oriented correctly.

She pushed the pyramid into the front of the suit and it nestled in with a click.

It was a perfect fit.

If she pushed the button inside the suit now, something just might happen.

Something bad to whoever, or whatever, she pointed it at.

She should rest and spend the night in the cave.

But life was all about taking calculated risks.

And she had waited long enough.

It was time to get her father, and finally get out of OZ.

Chapter 9

The flight back across OZ felt like it took no time at all. The last thing Caleb remembered was abandoning the automaton body of Dorothy in the wreckage of the crashed airship. The next thing he was aware of was stepping out of the Southern Marshal's airship onto the landing platform of her castle in the Southern Territories, hundreds of kilometers away.

The last several hours were nothing but a blur. He had been unable to hold on to any single thought for longer than the moment it took to think it.

As he stepped onto the platform, a frail old man in a wheelchair blocked him. He tried to step around the wheelchair, but the old man was surprisingly agile for being so thin and fragile. He spun the wheelchair around and blocked him again.

Enough with people always trying to get in his way. "Is there something I can do for you?"

The man looked up at him, sadness written on his face. "You have to help my daughter."

"Sorry. I'm out of the hero business."

He tried to step around the wheelchair again, but the man rolled over his foot and stopped him cold in his tracks. He yanked up on the wheelchair and pulled his foot out.

"What is your problem old man?"

"My problem is, you're the only one who can help me and you just told me no. I don't accept that answer."

"I'm not the only one who can help you."

"Yes you are."

"And why is that?"

"Because you're the only one who can get through to my daughter."

Caleb sighed. The only way to get rid of this old man was to appease him. He looked around at the other individuals on the platform. He didn't see a girl anywhere. "Okay. Fine. Where's your daughter?"

The man in the wheelchair gave him a quizzical look. "I was hoping you could tell me."

Caleb finally looked the man in the eyes. The eyes that looked back at him were familiar. They were the eyes of someone else he knew in the face of a man he had never met before.

The man pleaded with him. "That's right. Dorothy is my daughter. And only you can save her."

Caleb laughed at the absurdity of his comment. "Save her? She's an army of one in that suit you built. Nobody, and nothing, can touch her. What could I, possibly, save her from?"

"Herself."

Chapter 10

Less than an hour after speaking to Dorothy's father on the platform, Caleb stood on the highest balcony he could find at the Southern Marshal's castle. His hands gripped the railing and he closed his eyes as the wind ruffled the fur on his face.

His sense of loss was replaced by anger.

Anger at the Southern Marshal for lying to him.

Anger at Dorothy for lying to him.

Anger at himself for being distracted enough to believe the lies.

He should've been able to tell, by smell alone, the scarecrow version of Dorothy was not the real Dorothy. But he had spent so much time trying to get back to her, that when he finally did, or at least he thought he did, he eagerly accepted it as the truth.

He had been so lost in his self-deprecating thoughts, he hadn't noticed the Southern Marshal coming up behind him. He jumped a little when she spoke.

"I come up here often to ponder life's imponderables. I find the peace and quiet enables me to do my best thinking. Don't you agree?"

He wasn't happy with the intrusion into his private time, even by the Southern Marshal. "Yes, when it's quiet."

She either didn't pick up on his hidden subtext, or didn't care. She continued on in her easy conversational manner.

"I'm not in the habit of apologizing, and I'm not going to start now."

He didn't bother to mask the sarcasm in his own voice. "You sure do have a funny way of apologizing."

"Everything I do serves a purpose."

He turned on her. "What was the purpose in giving me a fake Dorothy? You didn't think I was going to figure it out sooner or later?"

She shrugged. "Given enough time, you would have figured it out. But the time we had was short, and you were distracted with the quest. I fully expected all of you to return. I would have disposed of the scarecrow Dorothy, and you would have been reunited with the real one, under the claim that her memories were restored. You quite possibly might never have found out."

"Why go through all of that?"

"Because of the genetic requirements, Dorothy and her father are the only two people in the world who can operate the Tin Man suit. It was actually Dorothy's idea to bring a clone of her along to keep you distracted."

"Well it worked. I fell hook, line, and sinker for your deception."

She didn't, nor did she need to, respond.

His eyes traced the distant mountain ranges. "She's out there, somewhere, with the ultimate weapon and wearing a powered armor suit that is slowly driving her mad. Unless, of course, you're lying about that too?"

"The Dorothy you knew could never have killed those men in cold blood. But the Dorothy inside that suit, is not the Dorothy any of us remember."

He shook his head. "Why even invent something that would take you to the brink of insanity, and then push you over the edge the more you used it?"

"I don't have an answer for that."

OZ seemed both too large and too small at the same time. Dorothy could be on the other side of the continent, or she could just be on the other side of those mountains.

The Southern Marshal rested a hand on his shoulder. "I know what you're thinking, but she wouldn't be just anywhere. I don't know where she is, but I do know where she will be. She's coming here."

Chapter 11

Caleb was simultaneously jerked left and right, and forward and back, as an entire crew of individuals tightened the straps to the thin, and overly light, armor that had been wrapped around him in successive layers. If he ever accepted his position as king over the hybrids, he would have to get used to being dressed by a gaggle of attendants. This whole experience was making him second-guess ever wanting to become royalty.

Benjamin Gale, Dorothy's father, rolled to a stop in front of him and held up a stubby brass key.

"This will force the Tin Man suit to open from the outside. It's an emergency safety release, should the operator be too injured to open the suit themselves. The keyhole is at the base of the neck on the back of the suit."

Caleb took the key and slipped it into the front pocket built into the suit of armor. "Wouldn't it have been better to make a suit that wouldn't drive her crazy?"

Benjamin didn't bother to respond.

Beyond his silence, there was still something he wasn't saying. The silence dragged out for a few moments until he decided to ask the important question.

"So, how do I get close enough to use the key?"

Benjamin seemed to be struggling with an internal conflict that didn't seem to fully resolve itself before he replied "I don't have anything that can disable the suit."

The realization dawned on him what Benjamin was actually saying. It wasn't good.

"I have to somehow get on the back of the Tin Man while she's trying to kill me?"

Benjamin waved his hands about in a chopping motion. "It's best to think of the Tin Man as a 'he'.

Dorothy's not the one doing this, the suit has changed her."

"Well, neither of them is going to make this easy."

"I didn't say this was going to be easy…"

He joined Benjamin mid-sentence as they both said, "but it has to be done."

Benjamin almost cracked a smile. Almost, but not quite.

"Dorothy said you were a bit of a smart ass."

"You should meet Jasper."

The group finished pulling him in all directions and backed away simultaneously without a word, as if they had done this many times before and didn't need to speak to know what they should all be doing.

Benjamin rolled backward to look him up and down. Now he smiled.

"How does it feel?"

Caleb flexed his arms, rolled his neck, and alternated standing on one foot and then the next. Despite how tightly the armor plating was strapped to him, he could move as freely as if he were naked.

He inspected the seams between the armor plates. The layering method the dressing crew had used did the job far better than he had expected. There was not a single part of him exposed, except his face.

As if they could read his mind, one of the dressing crew held up the faceplate that would snap into place to seal him inside the suit.

Benjamin seemed very pleased with himself. "Once the faceplate is secure, nothing can touch you. It uses the same flexible armor in the first suit I gave you, which you lost, but can withstand a greater impact due to the layering effect. And it is much lighter than any of my previous designs. You should have no problem holding your own against the Tin Man, but still have the agility to get behind him, use the key, and get my daughter out."

The Southern Marshal rushed into the room, flanked by six personal bodyguards on either side who did their best to keep up with her and still maintain a level of decorum.

She stopped in front of Benjamin, her guards snapping to attention as they stopped with her.

"She's here."

Chapter 12

The Tin Man suit was not designed for sneaking around or stealth operations. Why bother with any of that when the Tin Man was designed to withstand every type of conventional weapon known to man? And even some that hadn't been invented yet.

Forget about sneaking in to the Southern Marshal's castle. Dorothy could just walk, or more accurately crash, through the front gates and demanded the release of her father.

This is exactly what she did.

Smoke filled the air, along with the accompanying reports of gunfire, from single-shot flintlock pistols, all the way to large-bore cannons. All but the largest cannonballs were useless in slowing her down. Those, she made an effort to dodge after the first one knocked her flat on her back.

She didn't need to use her grappling claws to clear the way before her. Everybody who stood between her and the castle fired on her with all manner of weaponry until she got close. Then they scattered in all directions, leaving a clear path for her in the road ahead.

Getting to the castle was proving to be no challenge at all.

It was also no fun at all.

She had enjoyed killing the men who tried to keep her from the weapon. It was exhilarating. No, that wasn't right. It was…

It was liberating.

She felt free.

She felt powerful.

She had power.

The same power reserved for gods and governments.

She had the power over life and death.

She alone decided who lived and who died.

Without the Tin Man suit, she was at the mercy of everyone around her. She had been weak and had no choice but to trust everyone in a place filled with criminals.

She no longer had to trust anyone but herself.

That was freedom.

Her father warned her that spending too long in the suit would cloud her thinking.

It was just the opposite.

She was now thinking more clearly than she ever had before. She was indestructible and might never take off the suit again.

Chapter 13

Caleb used the roofs of the city to maintain a parallel course with the Tin Man...Dorothy. He couldn't separate the two in his mind once he found out it was Dorothy inside the machine. It was best to think of her as the Tin Man until she was separated from the suit.

She was, after all, the heart of the Tin Man. But that heart was being turned black by the very same machine that gave her strength. The only way to save her was to separate her from the Tin Man. Only then could she begin the road to recovery.

He finally understood what she was talking about when they were first back together at the Southern Marshal's castle. She had told him she needed someone she could trust to save her when no one else could. She failed to tell him he needed to save her from herself. And that she would try to kill him when he did.

With very little that could stop the Tin Man, or even slow him down, he was working his way through the city at a quicker pace than Caleb was. Caleb would have to run faster if he wanted to keep up with the death machine bearing down on the castle.

He slipped on a loose tile and his foot shot out from under him.

He landed on his side, his momentum propelling him forward toward the edge of the roof. He flailed his arms and legs, trying to catch some purchase with his hands or feet. He flew off the roof and dropped like a rock.

His suit hardened on impact and kept him from being killed after falling five stories, but colliding so sharply with the ground still stunned him for a brief moment. A crowd quickly gathered as he lay unmoving on his back.

He looked up at the faces that peered down from the crowd that huddled around him.

"Do you think he's dead?" someone asked.

His armored suit softened and he could move again. The crowd shrunk away as he rolled over to his stomach, up to his hands and knees, and stood again. He wobbled slightly as he re-calibrated his bearings and then took off running in the direction of the castle.

"Hey!" Someone shouted from the crowd behind him. "You dropped this."

A boy held up a stubby brass key, the same key he needed to unlock the Tin Man. He felt his front pocket. It was empty. The key had fallen out when he hit the ground.

He ran back and retrieved the key from the kid, losing precious seconds. Precious seconds that allowed the Tin Man to get closer to the wide open field that separated the castle from the surrounding city. If the Tin Man reached the field before he reached the Tin Man, he would never be able to sneak up behind him unnoticed.

This new suit he was wearing was agile and light, and protected him from blunt force trauma. But, unlike his previous suits, he had no integrated swords, no guns, and no jet pack. The only weapon he had was the element of surprise.

He would lose that if the Tin Man made it to the field first.

He gripped the key tightly; he wasn't going to trust that to the pocket a second time, and sprinted through the city.

He used the sound of echoing gunfire to gauge the location of the Tin Man. Ahead of him, the tallest spires of the Southern Marshal's castle were visible above the city rooftops. He kept running until he burst out of the city proper and into the open field.

The gunfire still echoed from inside the city.

Finally, things were looking up for change.

He had made it here ahead of the Tin Man.

Chapter 14

Dorothy strolled casually through the streets of the city toward the castle where her father was being held prisoner. The Tin Man suit deflected everything they shot at her.

They had fallen into a steady, if not redundant, rhythm. Defend, retreat. Defend, retreat. Defend, retreat. If her mission wasn't so serious, it would have been comical. Maybe someday she'd look back on all this and laugh.

The city opened up to reveal the Southern Marshal's castle on the other side of a wide open field.

Her voice sounded muted and hollow inside the suit as she spoke to herself.

"I'm coming for you, Father."

All the years wasted.

Her mother had died in her arms, and there was nothing she could do about it.

Every time she went out to find her father, she was returned to Aunt Em's farm, and there was nothing she could do about that.

She easily, maybe too easily, trusted everyone she met after crashing into the world's largest prison, only to be betrayed.

And there was nothing she could do about that either.

She felt the bulk of the Tin Man suit around her. The pain and discomfort she first experienced had shifted to numbness the longer she was inside. Her father warned her about staying in the suit too long.

He was wrong.

The suit wasn't just changing her. It was improving her.

Her father would see. She would make him see.

She would show him she was a better human being when she was the Tin Man.

She didn't need anybody else. She finally had someone she could rely on who would never betray her.

She had herself.

Nothing would stop her. Nothing could stop her. She was invincible now that she had the hybrid weapon integrated into the suit. A finger played with the button that matched the symbol on the pyramid. She looked at the burn on her hand and then across the field to the thick stone walls that protected the castle.

It was time to see just how much power she had.

She pushed the button and the clockwork mechanisms inside the suit twisted the capstone on the pyramid.

There was no loud sound. There was no blinding light. There was nothing at all.

But a section of castle wall crumbled to dust as if it had aged a thousand years in a second. She held her finger down until the hole in the wall was big enough for her to walk through unhindered. She released the button and the castle wall stopped breaking apart. A few pieces broke off and fell, but it was no longer aging before her eyes.

She looked again at the burn on her hand. Now that she had seen the weapon in action, she regarded her own hand with different eyes. It didn't look so much burned as it looked like that part of her hand was a hundred years old and her skin had begun the process of decay while she was still alive.

This weapon could alter the course of human history.

It's a good thing it was in her hands and not someone else's. At least she could control it.

Chapter 15

On a rooftop, just above the Tin Man, Caleb watched the castle wall crumble on the other side of the field.

That could mean only one thing.

She had figured out how to put the hybrid weapon into the suit, and use it. If Benjamin was right about the suit driving her insane the longer she stayed in it, whether or not she could control the weapon was beside the point. She would be unable to control herself.

That made her the last person who should have it.

From his vantage point, above and behind the Tin Man, he could see the keyhole at the base of the neck.

He couldn't hold the key in one hand and jump down on to the Tin Man from here. He fully expected a sudden and violent reaction and needed both hands to hold on once he was on the Tin Man's back.

He went to place the key between his teeth to hold it while he jumped down when it plinked against his faceplate. His armored suit allowed him to move so freely, he forgot he was wearing it.

He couldn't hold it between his teeth and he needed both hands free if he planned to stay on the back of the Tin Man.

He would have to trust the key to the pocket.

And he would have to trust he could fish it out of that pocket while holding on to a bucking Tin Man with one hand.

The most important thing was staying away from the hybrid weapon. The suit Benjamin gave him would protect him from everything, except a direct hit from that weapon. So no matter what he did, he had to stay behind the Tin Man.

Sounded easy enough.

He was committed to the jump, and had already leapt from the roof, when the Tin Man took a step forward.

Rather than landing on his back, Caleb hit the ground behind him.

He didn't land quietly.

The Tin Man spun around, swatting at him with a claw. His suit absorbed the impact as he flew backward, and the key flew out of his pocket to land somewhere in the tall grass.

He rolled quickly back to his feet and crouched, ready for the Tin Man's next move. A claw shot out at him on its extended chain, but he ducked low and rolled between the Tin Man's feet.

The Tin Man was surprisingly nimble and was already facing him as he got back to his feet.

The single, unblinking amber eye stared at him while he stared at the symbol of an eye etched into the center of the Tin Man's chest.

They faced off at the edge of the field, Caleb not taking his eye off the weapon pointed at him. With the key lost, his initial plan was out the window. The only way the Tin Man suit would open now was if she opened it. It was time to appeal to the girl inside.

He twisted off the face plate from his suit of armor and let it fall to the ground. If he was going to get through to her, he had to let her see his face. His eyes darted back and forth, searching for any way to see Dorothy inside the suit. All he could see was the Tin Man.

"Dorothy? Can you hear me?"

"Get out of my way Caleb."

"I want to help you."

"I have all the help I need."

"Come out of the suit, Dorothy. Let's talk about this."

"Once my father's out of OZ, I'll be happy to sit down and talk about whatever you want, but I will not ask you to move again."

Keeping his eye on the etched symbol on the front of the Tin Man suit, he watched for any sign that she was about to use it on him.

"I've spoken with your father. He's waiting at the castle for you."

"I know. That's where I'm going."

"Not like this, Dorothy. Come out of the suit. We can both get your father. Together."

"I need the suit to rescue my father."

"You've already rescued him. He's packed and ready to leave. The Southern Marshal even offered her fastest airship so the two of you can go anywhere you want."

"I don't believe you."

Well at least she said that, instead of killing him outright. He might be getting through to her. He stood up slowly and tried to look relaxed.

"I'm telling you the truth."

"I'm not giving this suit to the Southern Marshal. Nobody deserves to have access to a weapon this powerful."

"Right. And she doesn't want it. The plan has always been to take the airship out of OZ, fly over the nearest volcano, and drop the suit, and the weapon, into it. After that, the airship is yours, to go anywhere you want."

He gave that a moment to sink in. She hadn't moved or tried to kill him for nearly a minute now. The silence stretched on as they faced each other. The fact that she hadn't done anything was a good sign. He imagined the battle for control raging inside her mind. On the one side, the Dorothy he knew and loved, and on the other, the blackened soul formed by continued exposure to the suit. If he didn't get her out soon, he would lose her to the Tin Man forever.

The only sound, the tall grass rustling in the light breeze, was shattered by a thundering boom from the city.

The cannonball hit the back of the Tin Man and exploded. Caleb dove to one side as the Tin Man was shoved face first to the ground, plowing a meters long trough in the dirt from the momentum caused by the impact.

He watched in horror as the Tin Man stood back up, faced the city, and triggered the ancient hybrid weapon.

Laying down in the tall grass, he couldn't see what was happening to the city, but he could hear the screams.

He stayed low as he crawled through the grass, trying to stay out of sight and away from the eye of the weapon.

Content with the destruction she had brought down upon her aggressors, she turned her attention a little closer to home.

He could hear the grinding of gears as the Tin Man's torso twisted, searching the field for him.

Chapter 16

Caleb shuffled through the tall grass on his hands and knees, staying as low as he could so as not to be spotted. He thought of his ancestors in the African plains, crouching in the dry grass, stealthily sneaking up on their prey. Only he wasn't the predator this time. He was the prey, struggling not to be discovered.

He stopped every time he heard the Tin Man's gears stop. He could only move when the sound of the powered suit's own machinery masked his escape through the tall grass.

His hand nudged a small rock and he looked down. Maybe he could throw it in another direction to draw the Tin Man's attention and make a break for the temporary protection of the city. Temporary because that weapon could reduce the entire city to microscopic dust in a matter of hours.

He did a double take.

It wasn't a rock.

It was the brass key.

He snatched it up and clutched it close to his chest, clinging to it as if it were his only hope.

Which it was.

Now that he had the key, he could separate Dorothy from the Tin Man. Another clap of thunder echoed out from another part of the city. After bits of dirt and rock stopped raining down on him, he hazarded a peek through the grass, his heart thudding loudly in his ears.

The Tin Man was facing away from him, and leveling another section of the city.

This might be his only chance. Best not let it slip by.

This time he was the hunter readying to pounce on his prey.

With the faceplate missing, he was able to grip the key in his teeth this time. He just had to make sure he didn't swallow it.

He took three deep breaths, trying to slow his heartbeat, as the muscles of his back legs tightened.

He sprang out of the grass and landed squarely on the back of the Tin Man.

So, far so good.

He forced the key into the lock at the base of the neck and twisted. The Tin Man responded with a hiss of steam through cracks in the back of the suit. He clung on tightly as the Tin Man bucked around, trying to throw him off. The brass key snapped in half, leaving part of it in the lock. If what he'd already done did not open the suit, there was nothing else he could do now. The key was broken and the lock was jammed.

The muffled sound of Dorothy screaming echoed from inside the hollow Tin Man. It wasn't a frightened scream or a scream of pain. It was a hostile scream.

The back of the Tin Man popped open, throwing Caleb off.

With the seal on the suit broken, it began the shutdown procedure and leaned forward slightly as every internal mechanism ground to a halt.

Dorothy clawed her way out the back of the Tin Man and spotted Caleb.

She hissed like a cornered animal and launched herself at him, tackling him back down to the ground. He saw the blade in her hand a moment too late as she brought it down to stab him in the heart.

His layered suit hardened from the impact and prevented the blade from piercing him. She jabbed down repeatedly, but each time, the suit protected him. He grabbed her wrist as she slashed at his face, the only part of him not protected by the suit.

"Dorothy stop!"

She struggled against his iron grip. "Let me go!"

"Calm down. I'm on your side."

Her eyes bulged as she stared down at him, spittle foaming on the corners of her mouth. "My side!? You're just a pawn. Nero's pawn. He manipulated you just like he manipulated everyone else. I will not be a slave to him any longer. Not me! Not my father! Let me go!"

He tossed her off him as easily as tossing the covers off his bed each morning. She rolled to her feet as quickly as he sprang to his.

She held the blade in one hand, crouched, and growled like a wild animal.

He shook his head. "You want me to let you go?"

He stepped to the side and, with a flourish of his hand, motioned to the castle. "Fine! Go! But the suit, and the weapon, stays here."

Her eyes darkened. "And let you have it? I don't think so."

She sprang forward and slashed at him with the blade. He deflected her arm each time with his own.

She was relentless in her attack and he backpedaled with each jab and thrust of the blade.

How could she have changed so much? She was not acting like the Dorothy he knew at all. Had the suit pushed her to this in only a matter of days? Or had something happen to her during the months they were apart?

The Southern Marshal had done something to Dorothy. That had to be it. They had kept her from him for months, not telling him whether she was alive or dead.

And Nero was involved. He had to be.

Nero had been working with the Southern Marshal for as long as he could remember, so it hadn't surprised him when Nero showed up several days ago claiming to have found the hybrid weapon before losing it again.

It was never simple where Nero was concerned.

He had been so blinded by his reunion with Dorothy, he had forgotten about Nero's relentless pursuit of power. How nobody, and nothing, would stand in his way until he achieved it.

Maybe she was right. They had all been manipulated by Nero and his quest for ultimate power.

If they had any hope of stopping him, they would have to work together.

But that wasn't happening right now.

He ducked under her blade again and came up with a solid uppercut to her chin, stunning her and knocking her off her feet.

She hit the ground with a gasp as the blade disappeared into the thick grass.

She lay gasping on her back, trying to catch her breath when he stepped over her and held his hand out to help her up. "I am not your enemy. We will get your father. We will get both of you out of OZ.

And we will destroy the weapon. But if we are going to do this, we have to do it together."

The feral look in her eyes dissolved as she reached for his hand.

He pulled her up and hugged her tightly.

Her voice was muffled against his shoulder. "I'm so sorry Caleb."

He stroked her hair. "You had some valid points. I think there's something we can still do to keep this weapon from falling into the wrong hands."

Chapter 17

Caleb and Dorothy stood, arm in arm, patiently watching two airships descend on their position.

Before the airships touched the ground, ropes spilled from the gondolas and soldiers repelled down.

Caleb and Dorothy raised their hands in surrender as the soldiers surrounded them, guns at the ready.

Caleb did his best to put the soldiers at ease. "Relax fellas, we're all on the same team."

A swift kick to the back of their legs sent Dorothy and Caleb to their knees. Their arms were forced behind them and their hands bound.

"Whoa. That's a little tight there guys."

Once they were secured, one of the airships landed in the field and lowered its loading ramp.

The soldier behind Caleb grunted. "Alright, you two. Into the ship."

As they were lifted to their feet, Caleb nodded to the ground. "Could one of you fine soldiers be a gent and bring along my helmet?"

The soldiers looked at it, none of them making a move to pick it up.

"It's part of the special armor I'm wearing. The Southern Marshal will not be happy if it's left behind."

One of the soldiers nodded to another who bent down and retrieved his helmet.

As they headed up the ramp, he glanced behind and saw several soldiers tip the Tin Man on its side and begin the difficult task of hauling the heavy suit up the ramp into the other airship.

The trip back to the Southern Marshal's castle was made in silence. He and Dorothy were forced to sit at opposite ends of the gondola and were discouraged from talking.

Once they landed at the castle, he and Dorothy were split up.

He found himself in the same room where he had been manhandled into the layered suit of armor. His wrists were untied and one of the soldiers tossed his helmet to him, which he caught now that his hands were free.

The soldiers backed out of the room and closed the door, leaving him alone in the room, presumably with guards outside the door.

There was nothing left for him to do but sit and wait.

If he hadn't been paying attention to the incessant tick tock of the clock on the wall, he would've thought it had been longer than an hour before the door opened and the Southern Marshal stomped into the room, frothing at the mouth.

"Where is it?"

He let the look of confusion spread over his face. "I'm sorry?"

"You know full well what I'm talking about. Where is it?"

"Ummm… I'm afraid I don't know what you're talking about. Where is what?"

"There's an empty space in the Tin Man where the weapon should be. What have you done with it?"

He held his arms up so she could see his skintight armor. "You're welcome to search me if you like."

"You think I'm stupid? You won't have it with you. What did you do with it?"

"What could I have done with it? Your soldiers separated us right away. If somebody took the weapon, you might want to look at your own people."

"It seems you don't understand the position you're in. Why don't you save us both the hassle of torturing you and tell me where you buried it."

"I didn't bury anything. I don't have what you want. I don't have the weapon."

She snatched up his helmet from the chair by the door and felt around inside before tossing it back down on the floor. It bounced twice before rolling into a corner.

She narrowed her eyes at him, looking for any indication he was hiding something. "I'm glad you decided to do this the hard way."

She spun with a flourish and stomped back out the door. One of the soldiers leaned in and closed the door quietly.

Ten minutes later, the door opened again. Benjamin, Dorothy's father, wheeled in, his scarf tightly wound around his neck and face, leaving only his eyes exposed, but barely visible below the wide brim of his hat. He mumbled about how cold and drafty it was in this section of the castle.

A guard stepped in with him. Benjamin rotated his wheelchair in place and faced the guard, pulling the scarf away from his face.

"I'm just here to take back my armor. I don't think he'll be any trouble."

"The Marshal has ordered me to…"

"I don't care what she said. Only he and I know how to properly put on this armor. After the Marshal gets done with him, only I will know how to put on the armor, and that's how I'd like it to stay. Wait outside."

The soldier snapped to attention, saluted, and closed the door behind him, leaving the two of them alone in the room.

He twisted back around with a smile on his thin face. "Best idea I ever had, making the Marshal knight me as royalty in front of everyone."

His face turned serious. "We don't have much time. Do you have it?"

"When you first told me your plan, it sounded like a good plan. But that was before Dorothy and I were taken prisoner. You assumed we would be free to move about the castle."

Benjamin wheeled closer. "The plan is still good. We just have to improvise a little. Do you have it?"

Caleb lifted the couch and slipped the tiny pyramid out from under it. "I smuggled it inside my helmet and hid it as soon as I was alone."

Benjamin turned it over in his withered hands. "Everyone sure has gone to a lot of trouble for such a small thing."

"Small, but not insignificant."

Benjamin held it out to him. "Isn't that the truth? There's a compartment under my seat that will fit this perfectly. Strip off your armor. You will wear my clothes and sneak out past the guards pretending to be me. The armor piled in your lap should hide the fact that your legs are much stronger and bigger than mine."

Now that Benjamin's plan was in motion, Caleb worried about those they would leave behind.

"Come with us. If you stay, the Southern Marshal will kill you."

The old man shook his head as he unwound the oversized scarf from around his neck. "My days in OZ have been numbered ever since I arrived. I've managed to survive this long, and I think I can survive a little longer. At least long enough for you to get my daughter out of this godforsaken place and back to civilization."

"She won't leave without you."

"The airplane was designed to seat a single pilot with a little extra room for cargo. It's already a tight squeeze getting you both into it. Even if I could, we would be too heavy and the airplane would never get off the ground. The only hope of getting my daughter out of OZ means I have to stay behind."

"Then we'll figure out another way to…"

Benjamin patted the armrests of his wheelchair. "With this thing I would only slow you down. I'm counting on you, Caleb. You have to get my daughter home."

Benjamin had already made up his mind; that much was evident.

Caleb donned the clothes Benjamin had worn when he entered the room. Once the scarf was wound up around his face and the hat tilted down, unless someone bent down to look, they would not see the fur around his eyes. This crazy plan just might work.

Benjamin secured the pyramid under the seat of his wheelchair and wrestled himself onto the couch, refusing any help. He was proving that his decision was a decision not made from weakness.

Caleb sat in the wheelchair and piled the strips of armor into his lap. Placing them haphazardly around his lap, instead of neatly stacked, further hid the fact that he was not someone who needed a wheelchair to get around.

Benjamin looked him over and nodded approvingly. "There's just one thing left to do."

This was the only part of Benjamin's plan that Caleb was not particularly thrilled with. There were many things about Benjamin's plan he didn't like, but this part was the worst.

Benjamin motioned him closer. "I'm a fighter, Caleb. I'll be okay. Every success is built on sacrifice."

His heart thudded deep in his chest. "Does Dorothy know about this?"

Benjamin smiled. "Of course not. Now give me…"

Benjamin did not have the opportunity to finish his sentence. Caleb's balled fist collided with Benjamin's skull so hard, he heard his teeth rattle before he flopped unceremoniously off of the couch and onto the floor, unconscious.

For a moment, panic shot up his spine as he thought he might've hit the old man too hard. Then he saw the faint rise and fall of Benjamin's chest.

He breathed a sigh relief. Dorothy's father was still alive. He did not want to be the one to kill him.

He bent down and repositioned the old man, trying to make him more comfortable for when he woke up. He was going to have a splitting headache for a couple of days, that was for sure, but he didn't need any extra aches and pains from lying there awkwardly on the floor.

As he adjusted the old man, he spoke softly to him. "I don't think we can ever repay you for everything you've done to help us. Thank you."

Back in the wheelchair, Caleb banged it against the door. A guard started to open it when he shoved his way through, mumbling about how cold it still was on this side of the castle.

The other guard jumped out of his way before he rolled over his foot. He wheeled past them and around the corner.

Once out of sight, he abandoned the wheelchair and ran for the secret passage that would lead down to the airport hangar.

Was that the first left and then two right turns to get to the corner with the secret panel? He tried desperately to recall the directions hastily given to him when he skidded to a halt.

The pyramid!

He had left it in the wheelchair. He was so worried about getting away, all he could think about was how much faster it would be to run rather than use the wheelchair.

He spun back around and rounded the first corner back to the hallway where he had abandoned the wheelchair.

He collided with a soldier running the other way. They both went down hard, the soldier's rifle skidding across the floor.

Caleb rolled to his feet, snatching the rifle up at the same time, and brought the butt of the rifle down on the face of the soldier.

Lights out!

He skidded on his knees in front of the wheelchair and yanked the pyramid out from its hiding spot.

He vaulted over the fallen soldier as he ran back down the hallway and took the first left and the next two rights.

And stopped at a dead end.

It must've been the first two rights and then a left.

He ran back the way he came.

As he rounded the corner, a loud crack echoed in the hallway and a bullet ricocheted off the corner, spraying bits of shattered stone over his head. He fired two shots from the hip as he ran back around the corner. The soldier at the other end of the hallway responded with two more shots of his own.

He stuck the rifle around the corner and fired off two blind shots. That should keep the soldier held back for the moment.

He searched the hallway for any sign of the secret passageway, but there was no medieval suit of armor holding a spear that he could pull down on to open the passageway behind it.

This hallway was empty.

There were no doors or windows anywhere in the hallway. Just an empty space that terminated at a stone wall on one end. Why would anybody build a hallway that didn't go anywhere?

Another bullet ricocheted off the corner, reminding him of how bad his situation really was.

He was pinned down with nowhere to go.

Chapter 18

Caleb went over the directions again in his mind. He was sure it had been the first left, and then the next two rights. This had to be the place.

But where was the medieval suit of armor that would trigger the secret panel?

The hallway had been quiet for a little too long. Rather than peek around the corner and risk getting his head shot off, he poked the rifle around and fired off another two shots. The second shot resulted in a quiet click. He'd had only one bullet left, and he'd just used it.

It wouldn't take long for the soldier at other end of the hallway to figure that out.

He backed into the dead end and noticed an outline of dust in a rectangle shape on the floor. He inspected the floor more closely and saw scratches in the stone where something big and heavy had been recently removed.

This must be where the medieval armor had stood.

If this was the right place, then the secret panel was here.

He was on his hands and knees, studying and pushing down on each stone with his fingers. He pressed down on a tiny stone that was almost perfectly round and it sank with a click into the floor.

In front of him, the wall popped out and swung open like a door. The wall wasn't made from stone after all. It was a wooden door with thinly carved stone faces glued to it to match the full-sized wall stones on either side.

A volley of bullets chipped away at the corner behind him. Other soldiers had joined the first, and they were letting him know that they were coming.

By the time they realized he wasn't shooting back and charged the corner, he would be gone without a trace.

Chapter 19

Dorothy slid the wall paneling to the side and peeked out into the massive airplane hangar. As much as she wanted to pace back and forth to burn off some of this nervous energy, her hiding spot gave her little room to move.

Where were Caleb and her father? They should've been here by now.

If she had her Tin Man suit, she could go find them.

No. She had to stop thinking like that. Down that road was darkness, and death.

She was finally back in control of herself, and wouldn't let the suit take her back to a place she should never have gone in the first place.

The rhythmic pounding of someone running through the hanger echoed off the walls and ceiling.

She peeked out again and saw Caleb running toward the airplane.

Relief washed over her and she ran out to meet him.

They reached the airplane at the same time.

It was just Caleb.

"Where's my father?"

Caleb reached inside the cockpit and pulled on the choke.

"I'll tell you once we're in the air."

He ran around to the front and grabbed a propeller blade.

"Where is he?"

Caleb pulled down on the propeller and it spun to life, black smoke chuffing from the noisy engine. This new engine burned a flammable fuel and didn't require them to wait for it to heat up, or build pressure. As soon as it started, they were ready to go.

She took a step back and crossed her arms.

Caleb pleaded with her. "This plane was built for one person. We'll be lucky if we stay in the air with both of us in it. Your father knew that."

"That's not what he told me?"

"He told you what you needed to hear to get you on this plane."

She took a step backward, not liking the look in Caleb's eye. "I'm not leaving without my father."

A new voice echoed from across the hanger. "Hey! What are you doing?"

One of the Southern Marshal's soldiers, drawn by the noise of the airplane motor, raised his rifle when he recognized Caleb.

Caleb snatched her around the waist and pushed her ahead of him into the cockpit of the airplane. She went headfirst into the airplane as bullets pinged off the fuselage.

The same lead shielding her father had built into the plane to mask them from the perimeter defense system around OZ, easily deflected the bullets.

Caleb shoved the throttle to full with one hand and grabbed the flight stick with the other.

The plane surged forward and the soldier was forced to duck away from the propeller as they shot out through the open hangar doors.

The elongated wings lifted up at the tips as they gained speed.

Within seconds, the plane lifted off the ground and Dorothy's stomach somersaulted inside her body.

The ground fell away from them quickly and, after a couple of terror inducing maneuvers, Caleb quickly transitioned his theoretical knowledge of how to fly this plane into practical application.

Behind them, the Southern Marshal's castle receded until it looked like a dollhouse.

They were the fastest moving object in the sky. No airship could even match a third of the speed they had attained in less than a minute.

They had escaped, and nobody would be catching up with them.

Caleb shifted to one side so they were both sitting comfortably in the seat designed for one.

Caleb turned the plane, and the sun angled around until it was to their right. The closest way out, was to the south.

He pointed the plane in the direction of the small island of New Kansas that was hundreds of miles off the southern coast of the Australis Penal Colony.

Dorothy was finally getting out of OZ, but without her father.

She had not felt this way in a long time. The same emotions she had felt when her emerald heart necklace faded to black, the first time she had lost her father, swept through her again.

And just like that frightened little girl, so many years ago, she couldn't hold back the tears any longer.

Chapter 20

Caleb held Dorothy in the cramped cockpit and let her cry. He had watched over her since before she knew he existed, and he was glad to be here now. Glad to be the one to comfort her.

As they flew through the air, not a single word passed between them since they had taken off. The drone of the motor made talking difficult at best, so sitting together silently, in each other's arms, was the best thing for them.

A buzzer sounded, alerting him that they were getting close to the perimeter of OZ.

The lead shielding around the cockpit would mask their presence from the perimeter defense systems, but the engine on the plane was like a white-hot beacon that would get them killed if they didn't act fast.

He reached around Dorothy and gripped the engine release lever. Pulling this lever would shatter the ceramic bolts that held the engine in place and allow it to drop out of the plane. The elongated wings, and the thin cylindrical fuselage, would enable the plane to glide out of OZ un-powered, like a sea bird gliding on the updrafts along the shoreline.

He pulled back on the lever and the engine dropped away. The plane tilted up briefly before automatically leveling off.

Even without the noise from the engine, Dorothy nestled silently in his arms as they sailed over the southern edge of the continent and out across the crystal blue waters of the ocean.

There was still one thing left to do before they reached New Kansas. The original plan called for them to drop the weapon into one of the active volcanoes to the west of OZ. This gliding airplane would never make it that far, so the plan had to change.

Caleb held up the small pyramid.

Dorothy twisted sideways in the cramped space so she could face him. Without a word, she forced open the cockpit door just wide enough for him to throw out the pyramid.

He stuck his hand outside the plane, the wind buffeting the pyramid around, trying to knock it from his grasp.

One last look into Dorothy's eyes told him everything he needed to know. He smiled at her, and she smiled back.

He released his grip and let the ancient hybrid weapon fall away.

Despite the destructive power encased in the tiny pyramid, it made a tiny splash on the surface and sank quickly, disappearing into the depths of the sea.

He and Dorothy were finally free. They would land silently in New Kansas and, from there, go anywhere they wanted. As long as flowing cloaks with large cowls stayed in fashion, he could keep his feline features hidden from human eyes.

All he had to do was convince Dorothy that there was never a reason to return to OZ again.

Chapter 21

High up in the sky, in her own airship, the Banshee High Priestess held the telescope against her eye and studied the carnage on the ground below her.

Her arm was in a sling and several bandages clung to the side of her burnt face. If she had been but a single step to the left or to the right, she would have died with the rest of her Banshee warriors when the warehouse exploded. The concussive force had rattled loose the steel grate she was standing on, dropping her through the floor and into the sewer when everything else above her was reduced to rubble and smoke.

It had taken far longer to commandeer an airship, so she could pursue those responsible, than she had liked. It meant she was late to the party.

Everything that happened here was already a day old.

The airship that had crashed into the entrance to Chambers had effectively sealed it. But the bodies scattered around did not look like victims of the crash itself.

From her safe vantage point hundreds of meters in the sky she watched the still, and headless, bodies around the airship crash site; looking for an indication of where the hybrid and his robot went after they crashed into the entrance to Chambers. Being late was not much of a concern. She could pick up the coldest trail and follow it back to her prey.

If they survived the crash and subsequent massacre, only to go down into Chambers, they would be outside of her reach; for now. Even if they had escaped into Chambers, she wasn't worried. She had spies in every territory of OZ. If Caleb, or any of his companions, returned to the surface, she would know about it.

Unfortunately, most of her contacts, actually all of them, had fallen silent within the last twenty-four hours without warning. This was most unusual.

Even more unusual, the radio link she maintained with her spies reported nothing but static. Her hard-wired telegraph communications network still functioned, but it was as if something was interfering with her radio transmissions.

She was at the northernmost tip of the island continent of OZ. Maybe that had something to do with the radio. She was too far away to communicate with Center City. That had to be it. What else could be interfering with her radio?

The spotter, whose job it was to always scan the horizon, lowered her binoculars. "Ma'am? I think you better see this."

The High Priestess squinted in the direction the spotter pointed. At the edge of the horizon, tiny black dots, too numerous to count, filled the sky for kilometers in either direction.

She looked through her telescope and her heart nearly stopped.

Magnified, the tiny black dots resolved into hundreds of airships, each painted black with rows of cannons protruding from the sides of the gondolas.

Something wicked was coming to OZ.

Other Books by the Author

A is for Apprentice (Fantasy)

Oliver Twist: Victorian Vampire (Fantasy)

A Tale of Two Cities with Dragons (Fantasy)

Shade Infinity (Science Fiction Thriller)

Peacekeepers X-Alpha Series (Thriller)
> Inherit the Throne
> The Warrior's Code

Steampunk OZ Series (Science Fiction Serial)
> Forgotten Girl
> The Legacy's World
> Emerald Shadow
> The Future's Destiny
> The Dangerous Captive

Missing Legacy

Shadow of History

The Edge of the Hunter

Fugue: The Cure (Science Fiction Short Story)

Stay informed about all the trouble I keep getting into. Subscribe to Steve DeWinter's Book Report (i.e. the mailing list) @ SteveDW.com